THE NEED TO KNOW LIBRARY™

EVERYTHING YOU NEED TO KNOW ABOUT
SEXTORTION

AVERY ELIZABETH HURT

Rosen
YA™

New York

Published in 2018 by The Rosen Publishing Group, Inc.
29 East 21st Street, New York, NY 10010

First Edition

Library of Congress Cataloging-in-Publication Data

Names: Hurt, Avery Elizabeth, author.
Title: Everything you need to know about sextortion / Avery Elizabeth Hurt.
Description: New York : Rosen Publishing, 2018. | Series: The need to know library | Audience: Grades 7–12. | Includes bibliographical references and index.
Identifiers: LCCN 2017003114| ISBN 9781508174080 (library-bound) | ISBN 9781508174066 (pbk.) | ISBN 9781508174073 (6-pack)
Subjects: LCSH: Online sexual predators—Juvenile literature. | Extortion—Juvenile literature. | Internet pornography—Juvenile literature. | Computer crimes—Juvenile literature. | Internet and teenagers—Juvenile literature.
Classification: LCC HV6773.15.O58 H87 2018 | DDC 364.16/5—dc23
LC record available at https://lccn.loc.gov/2017003114

Manufactured in China

CONTENTS

INTRODUCTION

Cassidy Wolf had a lot going for her. She had been crowned Miss Teen USA and was preparing for a career in modeling or film. But she had no idea that she was being watched in her own bedroom. Shortly after receiving a notice that someone had tried to change Wolf's Facebook password and had hacked her Twitter account, she began to receive email messages containing nude pictures of her changing clothes taken from inside her bedroom and threatening to make public those pictures, along with tapes of private conversations between Wolf and her family. The person sending the emails wrote that he would turn Wolf's dreams of being a model "into being a pornstar" if she didn't send more nude pictures or a racy video or go on Skype and "do what she was told."

Amanda Todd was a seventh-grade school student in British Columbia, Canada. She met friends online and talked with them by webcam. One of the people she talked with plied her with compliments about her beauty and then asked her to show him a picture of her naked breasts. Todd trusted him and showed him her breasts. A year later, she got a message on Facebook saying "put on a show for me [or] I will send ur boobs." This person made it clear that he knew where Todd lived and who her friends and family were. She ignored him and hoped that would be the end of it. Then she found out that the picture of her breasts was making the rounds on the internet.

Ashley Reynolds was fourteen years old when she received an email saying that the sender had pictures of her naked and demanding more naked photos or he would send them to all her friends. Reynolds felt trapped. She sent more pictures, hoping the nightmare would go away, but it just got worse.

Wolf, Todd, and Reynolds are only a few of the thousands of young people—boys as well as girls—who have been caught in the snare of a cybercriminal known as a sextortionist. According to a 2016 report by the

Cassidy Wolf, crowned Miss Teen USA in 2013, didn't let her experience with a sextortionist stop her from reaching her goals.

United States Department of Justice, sextortion is "one of the most significantly growing threats to children." People who are caught in the sextortionist's snare feel trapped, as if they have no option but to cooperate with the criminal's demands. Some, like Todd, have been so devastated that they've taken their own lives. Others went to their parents and the police and asked for help, allowing them to put an end to the nightmare. These brave kids showed that there are several ways out of the sextortionist's trap and ways to avoid it.

Keep reading to learn about who sextortionists are, how they locate their victims, and what technical and psychological tricks they use to prey on those victims. Learn what to do if a sextortionist approaches and what protection there is from him, her, or them. There is no need to be afraid for yourself or someone who appears to be a victim because there is a solution to this problem, and you can help bring the culprit of such an act to justice.

CHAPTER ONE

TRAPPED

S extortionists use a variety of techniques to trap their victims. It's important to understand who sextortionists are, who they choose to prey on, and how they find those victims.

A VICIOUS CRIME

In Sir Arthur Conan Doyle's mystery novels, private detective Sherlock Holmes reserves his greatest contempt for a particular type of criminal: the black-mailer, sometimes known as an extortionist. In fact, Holmes said of Charles Augustus Milverton, a master blackmailer, "I've had to do with fifty murderers in my career, but the worst of them never gave me the repulsion which I have for this fellow." Sextortionists are criminals similar to the fictional Milverton, but they trade in sexually explicit material. Also unlike Milverton, they are often members of large crime syndicates and prey on young people who live in the digital world.

This teenager is looking at a website at home on her computer. Social media and other sites can be great for fun and education, but they must be used responsibly and with caution.

Sextortionists obtain private and sensitive material from their victims. Those materials might be nude photos, sexually frank text exchanges or audiotapes, or other media. Then, they threaten to make that information public or send it directly to the victim's friends and family members unless their victims send additional photographs or videos of a sexual nature, perform sex acts on camera, or in some cases meet the sextortionist in person and engage in sex acts in exchange for keeping the information or photos private.

According to the Federal Bureau of Investigation (FBI), once the sextortionist has a victim in his (or her) grip, he rarely lets go. He just continues to demand more increasingly sexual material. Victims can never be sure that a sextortionist has gone away—even if he is quiet for a long time. He can come back at any time with more threats and more demands—perhaps next week, perhaps years later.

SOFT TARGETS

Sextortionists prefer to target children and teens, and they prey on both boys and girls. According to a Brookings report on sextortion that used all known data up

This man is using the internet on his computer via a public connection. He may become the target of a cybercrime.

until April 16, 2016, 71 percent of victims are under eighteen years old, and some victims have been as young as eight years old.

One reason sextortionists so often single out young people is because, for this type of crime, kids are easier targets than adults. Young people can sometimes be naive and trusting. But more importantly, today's young people have grown up in a digital world. They are comfortable texting, posting on social media and forums, and meeting and chatting online with people, even people they've never met. This comfort level can cause young people to be less wary than they should be.

Sextortionists take advantage of these facts about how minors act. They scout their victims in chat rooms, on social media, and on online gaming sites, searching for young people who might be likely targets. They particularly seek out kids who spend a lot of time online, visit chat rooms frequently, overshare personal information, frequently post or discuss sexual or sexually related material, and share passwords or neglect other types of online security. The same Brookings report found that sextortionists used social media to scout for victims in 91 percent of the cases. They also used computer hacking in 43 percent of cases.

EXPERT SEXTORTIONISTS

It's not just lack of caution that gets kids caught up in the sextortionist's snare. These criminals are very good at what they do, and they can sometimes spend months setting their traps. After they've found a likely target, they might get to know him or her well over a long period of time. Often by the time the sextortionist makes his move, the victim doesn't even think of him as a stranger anymore.

One sextortionist, Lucas Michael Chansler, a thirty-one-year-old man who blackmailed more than 350 young people, pretended to be a teenage boy who was into skateboarding. He was so good at playing the role of a cool young skateboarder that his victims never suspected he wasn't who he said he was. When a poser like this asks girls for pictures of their breasts, the girls are often flattered that he wants to see them. Some may

HE DIDN'T SEEM CREEPY

Sometimes it can be difficult to tell if someone is trustworthy, even when you know who he or she is. One sextortionist who was later convicted and sent to prison sent phishing emails and hacked into hundreds of accounts. He sent email messages, containing young women's home addresses and details about what their houses looked like and how he might be able to get in, to the young women he was stalking—many of whom were aspiring models—so that they would know he could find them if he wanted to. You might imagine the man behind this scam working in a dark, grimy basement somewhere hunched over a computer and looking

(*continued on the next page*)

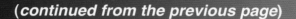

(continued from the previous page)

like the bad guy in a horror film. But in fact this man, Michael Ford, worked at the US Embassy in London. He did all of his computer hacking from his work computer at the embassy and stored some of the photos there as well. It's doubtful that anyone who worked with him had any idea what heinous crimes he was up to when they thought he was doing the country's business.

Michael Ford, former employee of the US Embassy in London (*pictured*), was found to have committed sextortion while on the job.

have thought of him as a boyfriend.

In another case, Robert Hunter, a thirty-five-year-old man from the United Kingdom, pretended to be Justin Bieber trying to get to know his fans. He convinced more than one young woman that he wanted to be her boyfriend. The same man who posed as Justin Bieber also tricked several boys into performing sex acts on camera by convincing them that he was a girl.

Sextortionists are also masters at psychological manipulation. The sextortionist who victimized Amanda Todd took advantage of her insecurity and convinced her to send him pictures of her bare breasts by repeatedly telling her how beautiful she was and that she should be proud of her beauty and not ashamed to share it. Sometimes, though, sextortionists seem to come out of nowhere. The victims may have never spoken to the person who suddenly sends an email for a text message demanding a ransom for photos.

BAITING THE TRAP

Though social media is the most common way sextortionists locate potential victims, they don't limit themselves to social media, and they don't always use persuasion and trickery to get compromising photos. Sometimes they just hack your computer or your social media account. Tech-savvy criminals can get into your computer or smartphone and access personal files and photos in a number of ways. One common way is by installing malware on your computer or smartphone, says ESET, an information technology security company. Criminals can do this without your ever knowing you've downloaded a program, much less a malware program. You might get an email that appears to come from someone you know, say a friend at school or

Cassidy Wolf is shown here accepting the Miss Teen USA award in 2013, after ending her ordeal with a sextortionist.

even a relative—it could be anyone you've ever emailed with. The subject line may say something like, "funniest cat video ever!!" or "have u seen this??????" There is a file attached to the email. You open the file; maybe there's a picture of a cat or maybe it's just some kind of placeholder: "Sorry this page is no longer available." You close the file and never think about it again. But this attachment is actually a program that is now installed on your computer, and it gives the criminal access to your computer whenever he wants it. He can search your files for photos or messages or other personal information and download them to his computer. The sextortionist can also install software on your devices that allows him to take control of the camera or microphone on your computer or cell phone so that you are being photographed or taped without you knowing about it.

That's what happened to Cassidy Wolf. When she

got an email showing her photos of herself naked, they weren't photos she had sent to a boyfriend or shared in a chat room. They were photos taken of her in her own bedroom while she was changing clothes. She had no idea someone had hacked into her computer's webcam.

THE TRAP IS SPRUNG

However he gets them, once the sextortionist has sexually explicit photos of a target, he gets in touch. He'll send a text out of the blue or maybe an email. He will tell the target that he has pictures of the target (or maybe some embarrassing text messages) and that he will post the material online (maybe even on the target's own Facebook page, if he's hacked that, too) or send them to everyone on the target's friend list if the target doesn't do exactly what he asks. At first his demands might seem mild. Maybe he has pictures of your nude breasts that you texted to your boyfriend or sent on a dare to other girls in school. So then he asks for a full-body nude picture. The victim may think that sending the sextortionist the full nude picture will convince him to keep the pictures to himself and leave the victim alone. He won't. Now he has even more damaging photos, and he'll use these to get progressively more sensitive material.

In some cases, sextortionists have not only threatened to share the photos but have threatened to physically harm their victims or victims' families if they don't get the cooperation they demand. Once a sextortionist has those pictures, the victim can never get them back, and he knows he has his target in his grip.

CHAPTER TWO

PRACTICE SAFE TEXT

t's fun to meet new people, and online forums and chat rooms are a great way to meet people from many different places. But someone can never be sure that the person on the other side of the conversation is who he or she claims to be. This doesn't mean that internet users have to completely avoid online chatting or posting on social media to be safe from predators. Just don't neglect caution and common sense when online.

SETTING BOUNDARIES

Set limits on what you will post before going online. Some necessary limits will preserve your privacy. Never share personal information, like your home address or your current location, with someone you only know through the internet. Don't post pictures of your home or your room online. Never say anything online or in an email or text that you wouldn't mind the rest of the world

Sharing a picture or text with the wrong people can be dangerous. For example, a person on vacation may reveal that his home is unoccupied.

seeing. Always take a few minutes to think before you post. It's easy to post a picture or a comment and then regret it later. Take time to be sure before you hit send. Anything you share online you have essentially given away. You can't get it back, you can't know who it will end up with, and you can't control what people will do with it.

If you're talking with someone online, and something doesn't feel right—maybe the person just seems creepy or is asking for too much information or is pressuring you to send photos—trust your instincts. Don't let friends or people you meet online pressure you or dare you to say or do or post something online that you're not comfortable with. You can just say, "Sorry, I'm not into that." You don't owe anyone explanations. If they keep badgering you, end the conversation and leave the website to create some space between that person and you. Tell your parents or another trusted adult what happened and why it bugged you.

Even though it can be fun to meet new people, the safest approach to online socializing is to accept friend requests and chat only with people you really know. Make sure you keep your social media accounts set to the strongest privacy settings, but don't assume that means you're safe. Anything you share with other people is on their accounts once you've shared it, and even if they are people you know and trust, they may not be as careful as you are with their social media accounts. Basically it's a good idea to think of anything you put online—words and pictures—as being written on the wall in a public place.

SAFE SIGN-IN

There are a few acts that can keep the information you put on a new account as safe as possible. Number one is to choose a good password. One sextortionist was able to get into his victims' social media accounts and home computers by guessing their passwords and security questions. It can be a challenge to come up with good passwords for all the sites you visit, but it is definitely worth the trouble.

According to the data security firm SplashData, the

two most common passwords of 2015 were "12345" and "Password." "Football," "Baseball," "Princess," "Dragon," and "StarWars" also made the top ten. To not become a victim, one must do better than that. Security experts offer the following tips for choosing good passwords:

- Choose a password with at least twelve characters, and mix it up between letters, numbers, and characters such as * or #.
- Don't use the same password for more than one site.
- Change your passwords often.
- Don't use personal information, such as your date of birth, street address, or middle name in your password.

Almost as important as the password are the security questions that sites often ask you to answer. Security questions seem like a good way for a site to make sure an unauthorized person can't get into your account. But they can sometimes make it *easier* for someone to hack your account. A common security question is "What was the name of your first grade teacher?" If someone knows your age and the town you live in, it's not hard to figure out who your first grade teacher was. Some security questions might seem harder to work out, but don't be so sure if you've ever discussed any of those topics online. Favorite TV character or singer? The city where your parents met? Grandfather's middle name? All of this information can be found (or guessed) by someone willing to do a little digging.

You can make up answers for security questions—

Creating an account online requires a password. This, along with other means of identity verification, is important to keeping other people out of an account.

your answers don't have to be true! Just be sure they aren't easy to guess but are easy for you to remember. Also, keep in mind that when you sign up for an online site or service, you don't have to give them all the information they ask for. Often sites will want to know a lot about you for advertising purposes. But you can usually leave some of it blank.

It's also a great idea to use two-factor or two-step authentication when you sign in to websites. With two-factor authentication, you not only have to provide something you know (your password) but also something you have with you, like a key card or a code from

PHISHING: NOT A DAY AT THE BEACH

Phishing is when someone sends a fraudulent email fishing for your private account information, such as your user name and password. It's easy to get hooked into phishing scams if you aren't careful. A typical phishing email will contain a link to a site where you have an account. It might say something like, "It appears that there was an unauthorized attempt to access your account. Please click this link to reset your password." So you click on the link and it takes you to a site that looks very much like the site where you have an account.

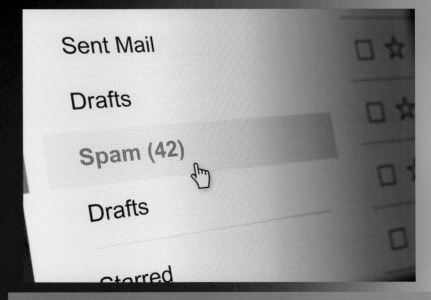

Email services attempt to filter out fraudulent emails. However, it is more important for a person to rely on his or her own discretion because it takes time for new senders to be recognized as spam.

(*continued on the next page*)

(continued from the previous page)

But it's really a fake, and when you try to sign in by putting in your username and password, the criminals who set up the scam get your username and password.

There are a few tip-offs that an email is not legit. If the email address doesn't match the sender, for example, it says it's from Yahoo!, but the sender address is yahooaccounts.com or hotmail.com or some weird site you've never heard of, it's a scam. In addition, phishing emails often contain misspelled words, poor grammar, or peculiar wording. For example, the text of the email may read: "Your account informations may have been under violation." If anything looks at all strange, close and delete the email. You can go directly to the site from the URL bar if you really have to go to Yahoo! or some other site you already know is legitimate. It's always safest to go to any site directly anyway. Hyperlinked text or a shortened link from widely accessible sites like Bitly and Ow.ly may be set up to deceive. Clicking on links like this is a common cause of trouble for many people.

a text message. Just guessing your password is not enough when a user relies on two-factor authentication, so it is harder for someone to break in.

THE DANGERS OF SEXTING

Sexting—sending nude, racy, or sexually explicit texts or photos electronically, usually by cell phone—has become common among teens in recent years. According to a 2012 survey of high school students that was published in the journal *Pediatrics*, 28 percent of the subjects had emailed or texted a nude picture of themselves, and over half had been asked to send a sext, though most of the teens who responded to the survey said they were "bothered" by the fact of being asked to sext.

The chances that sexy photos or comments will fall into the hands of a sextortionist make sexting extremely dangerous. Once they're sent, the sender can no longer control what happens to that picture. The way to be sure that sexy pictures do not end up appearing in public or being used against the sender is to keep them off of the phone or computer—especially off

Smartphones are the device of choice for teenagers and young adults. It follows that posting or sharing media through these devices cause them the most trouble.

someone else's devices.

Even if a sender trusts the person on the other end of a sexting correspondence to not share it with anyone else, that person can't be sure that another person—a sextortionist perhaps—won't get his hands on it later on. Phones and computers can be lost, stolen, and hacked. And a sour relationship can turn a trusted friend into a vicious adversary.

Sexting with a complete stranger is even riskier. You have no way of knowing who this person is or what he plans to do with your photo. Some of the people who were targeted by sextortionists thought that sending nude pictures to a stranger was safe—after all, they would never see him in person and never hear from him again. But they quickly learned how wrong they were.

There may also be legal consequences. Sexting between adults is generally legal, but sexting involving minors is illegal in all 50 states. Adults who send or keep sexually explicit photos of minors can be charged with child pornography or similar crimes. Most states, however, do not impose harsh penalties on teens who sext among themselves.

KEEP YOUR DEVICES SAFE

Sextortionists can install programs on their target's computer that allow them to access all of the files and even control its webcam. It's just like when the news shares stories about computer hackers who break into large hospitals, insurance companies, or political organizations and steal information—the criminals who do want your texts and photos can use the same techniques to break into your computer. You can keep the data on your home computer safe by taking some basic safety precautions.

The first rule of computer safety is to keep all your software up to date—especially your antivirus and malware-scanning programs. Computer hackers and software engineers are in something like an arms race. An operating system or program that was impervious to hackers last month might not be this month.

Never open email attachments you aren't expecting. If you get an email or a text from a friend that has a file attached, but you weren't expecting to get an attachment, do not open the file or reply to the email. Instead get in touch with the person the email was supposed to have come from and find out if he or she sent something. If not, immediately delete the email without opening it or the attachment. If you have already opened the attachment, run your computer's malware detection program to make sure you haven't downloaded a harmful program.

Don't download apps from websites or emails. If you want to install an app, buy it from the app store. And don't click on advertisements on websites or on flashing boxes telling you "you're the 100th visitor!" You haven't won anything, and you may lose a lot by following that link.

Taking these precautions should keep your computer safe, but still remember to close the top of your laptop when you're through using it, and put a piece of opaque tape or a small Band- Aid over the camera on your com-

A small piece of tape over a computer's camera can keep a hacker from spying on a user. That hacker may be a sextortionist or a different type of cyberstalker.

puter whenever you're not taking photos or videos.

It's a good idea to take precautions with your online accounts and electronic devices. But the way to be absolutely sure that a sextortionist doesn't get compromising photos or texts from you is to not have them in the first place. Something can't be stolen if it doesn't exist.

MYTHS AND FACTS

MYTH: Only your designated "friends" can see the things you post on social media sites, such as Facebook or Instagram.

FACT: Anything you put on the internet is potentially available to anyone. Privacy options may make content accessible to all, and shared posts widen the availability of what may have initially been shared with a small audience. And, compromised systems that sextortionists have broken into would allow direct access to material the owner thought was private.

MYTH: When you remove a picture or a post from your computer or social media site, it is immediately destroyed.

FACT: Throwing something away—whether on your own computer or on an internet site—doesn't mean the file is immediately destroyed, just that the space it takes up on the computer or server can now be used for something else. If it is online, it might be a long time before the information has been obliterated so that no one can get to it anymore—if a site doesn't simply archive deleted content in a place the user can't access. The safest bet is to assume that anything you post online exists *somewhere* forever. As for files on a computer, it is possible to extract permanently deleted information, so it never really goes away.

(continued on the next page)

(continued from the previous page)

MYTH: If several of your friends know someone online, he's probably safe.

FACT: Sextortionists often target groups of people. Getting to know several people who are friends helps them gather information (such as where you go to school or what kind of music you like) they can use to hack your accounts. Just because your friends talk with him, too, doesn't mean he's who he says he is. And it doesn't mean their relationship with the mysterious character is any different from yours with that person.

CHAPTER THREE

YOU'VE GOT MAIL

What if it's too late, and the sextortionist has sent an email or text demanding more photos? When this happens, people often think they are trapped and that they have no other option than to cooperate with the sextortionist. That's exactly what the sextortionist wants them to think.

DO NOT COOPERATE

The way any type of blackmail or extortion works is that the perpetrator convinces the victim that the only option is to do want the perpetrator says. But the truth is that there are other options. If the victim doesn't cooperate, then the extortionist doesn't succeed. Either he gets nothing (if he is ignored) and he retaliates, or he gets caught (if the targeted person goes to the police). He's pretty sure his victims will cooperate because if they don't, he will release some or all of the photos (or other kind of material) he has, and he expects that they are desperate for him not to do that.

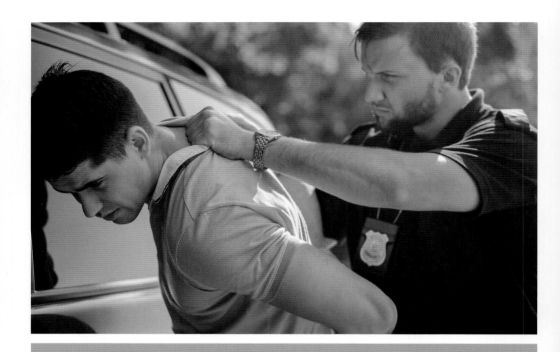

Sextortionists are often caught and prosecuted when their victims refuse to play the game and go to the police instead.

Sextortionists make money selling pictures like these on the black market. They don't want these pictures for their private collections, even if they tell you they do. The pictures you send a sextortionist, hoping that he will keep them private, are thus very likely to end up on any website that allows posting photos. And sending more pictures increases the amount of embarrassment that uncovering them can cause the victim.

It's not easy to refuse to cooperate—especially when the sextortionist doesn't seem to be asking anything very different from what he already has. And it's certainly no fun to have your pictures plastered all over the internet.

But cooperating leads to his demands becoming more serious. The sextortionist is counting on the fact that the deeper in you get, the harder it will be to get out. Ultimately, a sextortionist distributing the original photo is nothing compared to the terrible situations a victim could become involved in by cooperating with the disturbing demands of a sextortionist.

But just ignoring the requests is a bad idea, too. If you've been caught in a sextortionist's trap, you need to get help. And the good news is that help is out there.

CALL FOR BACKUP

Sextortion is a serious crime and sextortionists are dangerous people. If someone got to know this predator while he was pretending to be a handsome young skateboarder who constantly complimented the victim's appearance, it might take a while to realize that he's not just a teenager who might be talked out of sextortion. The truth is he's probably a professional criminal. According to Interpol, individual sextortionists often work for very sophisticated organized crime groups. These organizations sometimes even offer bonuses and incentive pay to the best-performing blackmailers. Sextortionists themselves are heartless. According to a Brookings Institute report on sextortion, one victim wrote to the person who was doing the blackmailing, "Please remember im[sic] only 17. Have a heart." The sextortionist responded with "I'll tell you this right now! I

National and even international agencies, like Interpol, become involved in investigating certain sex crimes, particularly those involving children.

do NOT have a heart!! However I do stick to my deals! Also age doesn't mean a thing to me!!!"

Once someone has demanded more photos or videos, the victim is in too deep. The best, safest, and wisest thing to do is to confide in either the victim's parents or another trustworthy adult. This may be hard to do, but it's surprising how reasonable and understanding parents are when it's a matter of safety. In an article about sextortion posted on the FBI's website, FBI agent Larry Meyer said, "You might be afraid or embarrassed to talk to your parents, but most likely they will understand." Meyer said that in his experience, parents have wished their children had told them sooner. Explaining the problem to parents will lead to them figuring out what to do to end the sextortion. They don't want their children to be victimized because of a bad decision. They don't want mistakes to ruin their child's life. Seeking help offers relief because the victim will no longer be dealing with this alone.

BREAKING THE NEWS

No matter how upset your parents may be that you broke their rules about sexting or talking to people online, they will almost certainly be your best allies when it comes to getting you out of the situation and keeping you safe. Don't let embarrassment keep you from telling them exactly what is happening. The people who are trying to help you need to know all of the details. Here are a few tips for making the talk a little easier:

• Sit down with your parents and let them know that you need to have a serious conversation. It might seem easier to just drop the news while riding in the car or washing dishes, but they will probably take the news better if they know to expect something serious.

• Start the conversation by telling your parents that you know you need their help and are counting on them to be there for you.

(continued on the next page)

(continued from the previous page)

• If one parent is easier to talk to than the other, you may want to go to that parent first, but don't keep any details from either parent. They both need to know everything so that they can both help you.

• Sometimes the best way to deliver bad news is to jump right in. Don't beat around the bush; just tell them what happened.

• Have this book or an article about sextortion with you so that you can explain to your parents what sextortion is all about if they don't understand what you're trying to tell them.

Turning to parents for help is almost always a huge relief for minors who are being preyed upon by sextortionists. Seeking help is the beginning of the end of the sextortion nightmare.

If you really don't feel safe talking to your parents about this, think about another adult in your life that you do trust—perhaps an aunt or uncle or older sibling. There may be a sympathetic teacher at your school, or perhaps you could confide in your school's guidance counselor. The important thing to realize is that this is a very serious situation, and you really do need an adult's help. Most adults, once they know what is going on, will be understanding and willing to help. However, if there is no one in your life you trust to help you with this, there is still somewhere to turn where you know they will understand the trouble you are in.

YOU'RE NOT ALONE

It's a good idea to get in touch with the police to report this crime. Even though it can seem very scary to go to the police or the FBI, when people report sextortion to the authorities, they feel a huge amount of relief. It is comforting to know that you are not the only person this has happened to. In fact, most people who were victims of sextortionists have gone on to live normal lives.

The authorities can find the sextortionist and stop him from harming you or anyone else. If you can't bring yourself to tell your parents about the sextortion, you can go directly to the police instead of relying on them to do it.

Local police will know how to get in touch with national authorities who are working on cases like yours. If you are in the United States, you can also go directly to the FBI by calling 1-800-CALL-FBI, or in either Canada or the United States, you can call the hotline of the National Center for Missing and Exploited Children (NCMEC) at 1-800-THE-LOST. When you call one of these numbers, or go to your local police, they will put you in touch with people who know exactly what to do to get you out of this situation and help you put your life back together as quickly as possible.

The FBI is also interested in hearing from people who were victims of sextortionists that have already been caught and put behind bars. They haven't been able to locate all of the victims, and they would like to find them so that they can put their minds at ease by

The FBI is eager to work on crimes that have a national scope or that are particularly uncommon to a municipality. A local law enforcement office often contacts the FBI when they determine that they need to.

letting them know that the sextortionist who preyed on them has been arrested and jailed. If you were contacted by a sextortionist but haven't heard from him recently, the FBI may be able to help you close this difficult chapter of your life.

TEN QUESTIONS FOR AN FBI AGENT

1. If I call the police to report a sextortionist, can I be arrested because I texted or emailed the original photos?
2. A friend of mine has been targeted by a sextortionist, and I think she is planning to cooperate with him. Is there some way I can help her? Should I call the police on her behalf?
3. If I cooperate with the sextortionist, will I be in trouble if I later tell the police?
4. If I report this to the police, what is the next step? What will they ask me to do? Will they confiscate my computer?
5. If I report the crime and they catch the guy, will I have to go to court?
6. The person who is asking me for more pictures is a grown-up I know in real life. I can't believe he would really do something to hurt me. What should I do if I don't want to cooperate but don't want to get him in trouble?
7. I'm almost certain there weren't any naked pictures of me on my computer, and I've never sexted with anyone or posted anything online. But this guy keeps saying he has something. Does he really? How can I know for sure?

8. I think the guy who is blackmailing me is just a kid. Should I still report him?
9. It's too late. I already sent him more photos. How can the police help now?
10. What have other kids done to help them cope with this?

CHAPTER FOUR

FREE

The previously mentioned stories of the young women who were the victims of sextortionists are very disturbing. They each had the potential to end like Amanda Todd, with a life ended. But Cassidy Wolf and Ashley Reynolds—and many other victims like them—made a different decision. They realized that suicide was not an ideal solution and that they didn't have to remain victims for the rest of their lives. Instead, they chose to do what was necessary to end their nightmare in a happier fashion.

Wolf and Reynolds discovered something when they went to the police and cooperated in the investigation of the crime: they were no longer victims but strong people who were helping to stop a dangerous criminal and save others from falling prey to sextortionists. It wasn't easy for them to tell their parents and to talk with the police about what had happened. Stepping forward was both embarrassing and scary. But it came as a huge relief to put the problem in the hands of professionals who knew how to handle the situation.

Victims often feel very alone. But when they go to the police, they learn that there are many others who've been caught in the same trap.

Reporting the crime is the only way to stop it and break free. Police can't catch sextortionists, and victims cannot recover if those victims do not come forward.

THE DAMAGE OF SEXTORTION

The effects of sextortion can be devastating and can last long after the experience is over. It's easy to assume that because the sextortionist did not physically harm the victim, the crime is not all that damaging. But the fact is sextortion can cause great harm to the victims. The Brookings report on sextortion describes it as "brutal" and considers it a type of virtual sexual assault. Reynolds described the experience in a *Glamour* article: "I felt like I was being virtually raped," and others victims quoted in FBI reports say they felt like "slaves." One court record that was cited in the Brookings report on sextortion described the crime as causing "unimaginable harm" to its young victims. The trauma can be as devastating for many sextortion victims as it is for people who have been physically violated.

Here is what that harm looks like. The long-term effects of having been a victim of sextortion include depression, loss of self-esteem, and a feeling that one is never safe, even in one's own home. Other effects are of a more social nature. If a sextortionist posts a person's pictures on the internet, then that can create a permanent footprint that will harm the reputation of the victim. Anyone can access those photos, and especially malicious people might distribute them even further or in places that are especially likely to be accessed by the peers of the victim. This can spiral downward even further when the act of sextortion is transformed from an encounter with a stranger to backlash from a hostile community or to lost professional opportunities because of the tarnished reputation.

REAL, POSITIVE OUTCOMES

Wolf said in interviews with news magazines and on television that when she got the email from her sextortionist telling her that he had nude pictures of her, she began crying and screaming and threw her cell phone at the wall. She was terrified, she said. She wasn't sure what to do, but she knew she needed help. She first went to her mother, and they contacted the police together when the sextortionist contacted her again. They also contacted the FBI on the following day.

Reynolds, only fourteen at the time a sextortionist got in touch with her, didn't seek help so quickly. She played along with her tormentor, meeting more and more of his demands, hoping that sooner or later he would just go away. By the third month, it was clear that he wasn't going anywhere. Reynolds felt that she couldn't confide in anyone. It was "the most alone I'd ever felt in my life," she later told a reporter from *Glamour* magazine.

Reynolds didn't know it, but in one way, she was far from alone. The same sextortionist who was preying on her was also tormenting 350 other young victims.

Reynolds began to feel that killing herself was the only way out. Fortunately, Reynolds's mother was using Reynolds's computer one day when she stumbled upon one of the emails to her daughter demanding more pictures. When she asked Reynolds about it, Reynolds told her everything.

Reynolds and her mom called the CyberTipline of the National Center for Missing and Exploited Children and got the help they needed to report the crime. The first step, according to the advice from the NCMEC, was to stop all contact with the sextortionist. Then, they should to get in touch with the police.

John Walsh (*pictured*), host of *America's Most Wanted* and cofounder of the National Center for Missing & Exploited Children, is announcing an extension to the Amber Alert system at the National Press Club.

At first Reynolds still did not want to call the police because she was afraid that she might be arrested for sending the sextortionist the pictures and cooperating with him for so long. Soon she realized that wouldn't happen; she was the victim of a crime, not the criminal. Her parents were very understanding, and she was incredibly relieved that she didn't have to carry this burden alone anymore. Though the sextortionist did post some of Reynolds's photos, that was minor compared to what he had been putting her through. He no longer had any hold on her. And because the sextortionist posted the photos, the FBI was able to trace the photos back to him. Lucas Michael Chansler, the criminal who was tormenting Reynolds—and hundreds like her—was arrested, prosecuted, and put in jail because Reynolds reported him to the police. Reynolds told *Glamour* that when she saw her abuser sentenced, she "felt empowered." Her nightmare was over.

Michael Ford, the man who ran his sextortion operation out of the US Embassy in London, was caught when an eighteen-year-old victim fought back. Because he had hacked into her computer, he had contact information for her friends and relatives, as well as compromising photos. He told her that if she didn't cooperate with him, he would send her nude pictures to her parents and her friends. She begged him to leave her alone. He didn't. When she threatened to go to the police, he wrote, "I gave you a chance, and you blew it." But it turned out that Ford was the one who blew it. His victim did go to the police, and soon Ford was caught, arrested, and sentenced to prison.

Because these victims were brave and willing to go to the authorities for help, they saved themselves and many others. Sextortionists typically have hundreds if not thousands of victims, and bringing just one of these criminals to justice can save many lives from being ruined.

These victims haven't stopped with just bringing the perpetrators to justice. They are now working hard to inform and educate other young people about sextortionists and explain to others what to do to make sure they don't become victims. Wolf speaks to teens and young adults about sextortion. She shares her story and offers advice about how to keep it from happening to her audience. Reynolds is also a successful and happy adult now and uses the story of what happened

Erin Brady (*left*) and Cassidy Wolf (*right*) educate other teens about the dangers of sextortion at the sixth annual Shorty Awards in 2014.

to her when she was fourteen to educate others about the issue and help them avoid the same trap.

Even though it doesn't always seem so at the time, victims of sextortion can go on to live happy, successful lives. But they still may need a little help with coping.

CHANNELS OF RELIEF

The victim of a sextortionist, even from a long time ago, should plan for the various aspects of the experience that may continue to cause harm. The plan he or she comes up with should involve a way to neutralize the sextortionist, remove and destroy damaging media distributed throughout the internet, and cope with the damage done to one's social life and emotional state.

For pursuing the sextortionist, every case is different, but the options will be either the authorities prosecuting the crime committed against the victim or the victim suing based on a civil violation. Consulting law enforcement will help the victim learn if prosecuting charges that may include extortion, soliciting and/or distributing child pornography, soliciting a minor, harassment, and others would be successful. The result of a successful prosecution would be any or all of the following: jail or prison time for the sextortionist, a fine, an injunction to remove any shared media from the internet or complete some other means of reducing the harm the sextortionist caused, and an order to not use the internet.

Going the route of suing for a civil violation like intrusion of solitude, appropriation of name or likeness, or public disclosure of private facts has different outcomes based on what the plaintiff asks for. Remedies in civil court might include demanding the culprit to take responsibility for any or all aspects of the violation, monetary damages, and, in what would probably be of greatest relief for the victim, an injunction to delete any uploads of the damaging material and destroy it.

If the sextortionist has shared photos or other media, there are a few options for making those sensitive materials unavailable. Contacting the site administrator and alerting him or her of a breach of the privacy policy can be one way to remove the media from the internet. If the site is unwilling to address the abuse, the police in a criminal investigation or the victim in a civil lawsuit can request an injunction from a judge for the website or the sextortionist to remove the media.

PERSONAL CARE

Throughout the process of seeking justice and after, it is essential for the victim to take care of his or her mental health. Social workers with the police department can put victims in touch with mental health care professionals to help evaluate if the victim is coping well. Or a victim may want to ask a school guidance counselor or minister to help with finding a professional who can help. Some professionals and services that would be beneficial to engage with are psychotherapists, group therapists, support groups for survivors of sex crimes or cybercrimes, or other types. Any type

DON'T IGNORE THIS

The victim of a sextortionist may have some lingering issues. But not all of the signs of distress are obvious. The sooner a victim seeks out help, the easier it will be to heal—and the sooner that person can be done with this nightmare. There are a few signs that might indicate that you or a person that you know who has been victimized needs help coping. If any of the following things are happening, talk about it with an adult you trust, and if you are the one who is suffering, try to arrange to see a counselor or psychologist:

A good counselor can be very helpful in coping with the long-term effects of sextortion.

- A victim can't seem to stop thinking about what happened.
- A victim has trouble thinking clearly or focusing on a task, such as schoolwork, reading, or a conversation.
- A victim is afraid to go out in public.
- Headaches, stomachaches, or colds or other minor illness occur more often than they used to.
- A victim has trouble sleeping.
- A victim's appetite has changed—either eating a lot more or a lot less than before.
- A victim's grades aren't as good as they were before the sextortion happened.
- A victim begins having trouble getting along with family and friends, often having arguments.
- Friends and family members have said that the victim seems "off" or that they are worried about that person.
- Things that used to be fun—going out with friends, riding bikes, watching movies—don't really interest the victim anymore.
- Being jumpy or overreacting to small things like sudden noises or interruptions.
- The victim has a lot of trouble trusting anyone—even the people that person knows loves him or her.

of one-on-one support would cost more than group support, but a victim must also take into account his or her comfort level with sharing the painful story of surviving extortion with other people.

A less institutional approach to self-care that can work in conjunction with some type of professional help is individual activity. Exercising regularly, eating a balanced diet, and taking time to enjoy hobbies would be a great way to affirm a victim's existence and appreciate that sextortion perhaps hasn't completely ruined everything. Meditating, trying out yoga, and doing breathing exercises can clear one's mind of stress. And playing sports or joining a new club can offer an outlet that doesn't attempt to directly engage with the trauma of surviving sextortion.

Emerging master blackmailers have tools that Charles Augustus Milverton, Sherlock Holmes's enemy, could never have dreamed up. But their victims have tools, too. They can protect themselves from modern-day predators, and if victims are caught in a snare, they can reach out for help and find relief. Sextortion is indeed a nightmare for its victims. But it is a nightmare that can meet its end.

appropriation To treat a person's name or physical likeness as an endorsement for a product or service. Appropriating without permission from the so-called endorser is illegal.

arms race When two parties compete to develop increasingly more powerful weapons that evade the other's defenses, often used metaphorically.

assault To attack someone in a physical manner.

attachment A file that is sent in an email.

blackmail To threaten to share information about someone if that person doesn't pay money or cooperate with some other demand.

black market An illegal system of trading goods and services.

confiscate When a government or other authority takes someone's property by legal means.

cybercrime Crime that is committed by using the internet or some other network.

download To copy a file from a website on the internet or another network to a computer or digital storage device.

explicit A graphic depiction, in words or pictures, of sexual activity.

exploitation The act of taking advantage of a person or situation.

extortion The act of using threats to get money or some kind of favor from someone.

fraudulent An act, practice, or item that is false or designed to deceive.

hack To gain access to an electronic device (such as a computer or cell phone), website, online account, or network to cause damage or reveal digital security vulnerabilities.

harassment To be pushy about involving someone in a matter that someone has already expressed a desire not to participate in but only when that someone should reasonably be able to choose whether or not to participate. Repeatedly asking someone for a lift to a concert is harassment, but telling someone to stop following another person is likely a reasonable request no matter how many times it is made.

Interpol International organization that coordinates the efforts of police departments in more than one country when investigating international crimes.

malware Malicious software; software designed to damage or disable a computer or to allow unauthorized parties to gain access to the computer and/or its files.

operating system The main software on a computer that makes it possible for the computer to start, run tasks that are essential to continuing operation, run other software, and shut down.

perpetrator A person who commits a crime; a culprit.

pornography Photographs or text that depicts naked people or sexual activities.

social media Online communities in which users can engage directly with each other by posting text, photos, and videos or by having conversations via chat or video chat.

FOR MORE INFORMATION

Boost Child and Youth Advocacy Centre
890 Yonge Street, 11th Floor
Toronto, Ontario M4W 3P4
Canada
(416) 515-1100 ext. 59338
https://boostforkids.org/programs/internet-child
   -exploitation
This center works to end abuse in the lives of young
   people's families. It also offers referrals for short-
   term counseling to children and teens who have
   been victims of internet abuse.

Family Online Safety Institute (FOSI)
400 7th Street NW, Suite 506
Washington, DC 20004
(202) 775-0158
https://www.fosi.org
This institute works to provide kids and their parents
   with the tools and education they need to be safe
   online. FOSI also educates government, the media,
   and industry professionals about balanced policies
   regarding internet safety.

Kidsafe Foundation
5944 Coral Ridge Drive
Suite #241
Coral Springs, FL 33076
(855) 844-7233
http://kidsafefoundation.org

Works to protect children from sexual abuse, bullying, and internet dangers by providing educational resources to children, parents, and educators.

National Center for Missing & Exploited Children

Charles B. Wang International Children's Building
699 Prince Street
Alexandria, Virginia 22314-3175
(800) 843-5678
http://www.missingkids.com/home
This organization provides services and technical assistance to children who are victims of abduction and sexual exploitation.

National Children's Alliance

516 C Street NE
Washington, DC 20002
(202) 548-0090
http://www.nationalchildrensalliance.org
This professional organization helps local communities respond to allegations of child abuse by putting the child first.

Teen Line

Cedars-Sinai Medical Center
PO Box 48750
Los Angeles, CA 90048-0750
(800) 852-8336 or (310) 855-4673
Website: https://teenlineonline.org
A nonprofit organization that helps troubled teens address their problems. The online support group

puts teens in touch with teens for education and support, with the aim of preventing problems before they reach the crisis stage.

WEBSITES

Because of the changing nature of internet links, Rosen Publishing has developed an online list of websites related to the subject of this book. This site is updated regularly. Please use this link to access the list:

http://www.rosenlinks.com/NTKL/sextortion

FOR FURTHER READING

Cindrich, Sharon. *A Smart Girl's Guide to the Internet.* Middleton, WI: American Girl, 2009.

Colt, James P. *Cyberpredators.* New York, NY: Chelsea House, 2011.

Klein, Rebecca T. *Frequently Asked Questions about Texting, Sexting, and Flaming.* New York, NY: Rosen, 2012.

Minton, Eric. *Online Predators and Privacy.* New York, NY: PowerKids Press, 2014.

Minton, Eric. *Online Passwords and Security.* New York, NY: PowerKids Press, 2014.

Minton, Eric. *Spam and Scams: Using Email Safely.* New York, NY: PowerKids Press, 2014.

Mooney, Carla. Online Predators. San Diego, CA: Referencepoint Press, 2011.

Mooney, Carla. *Online Privacy and Social Media.* San Diego, CA: Referencepoint Press, 2014.

Palmer, Libbi. *The PTSD Workbook for Teens: Simple Effective Skills for Healing Trauma.* Oakland, CA: New Harbinger, 2012.

Willard, Nancy E. *Cyber-Safe Kids, Cyber-Savvy Teens.* San Francisco, CA: Jossey-Bass (Wiley), 2007.

Botelho, Greg. "Arrest Made in Miss Teen USA Cassidy Wolf 'Sextortion' Case." CNN, September 27, 2013. http://www.cnn.com/2013/09/26/justice/miss-teen -usa-sextortion.

Brody, Liz. "Meet Ashley Reynolds, the Woman Fighting Extortion." Glamour, July 7, 2015. http://www .glamour.com/story/ashley-reynolds-the-woman -fighting-sextortion.

Brown, Pamela. "FBI: Sextortion a Growing Threat." CNN, July 8, 2015. http://www.cnn.com/2015/07/08 /politics/fbi-sextortian-growing-threat/.

Doyle, Arthur Conan. "The Adventure of Charles Augustus Milverton." *The Complete Sherlock Holmes.* Volume 2. Garden City, NY: Doubleday, 1930.

Gibson, Caitlin. "They Call It Bunny Hunting." Washington Post, September 6, 2016. https://www .washingtonpost.com/lifestyle/style/they-call-it-bunny -hunting-how-authorities-warn-kids-about-online -predators/2016/09/06/2044ee40-5980-11e6-9767-f 6c947fd0cb8_story.html?wpisrc=nl_evening& wpmm=1.

Heller, Zoë. "'Hot' Sex & Young Girls." New York Review of Books, August 18, 2016. http://www.nybooks.com /articles/2016/08/18/hot-sex-young-girls/?utm _medium=email&utm_campaign=NYR%20Girls %20wildlife%20fashion%20science &utm_content=NYR%20Girls%20wildlife %20fashion%20science+CID _077fec5921a0029075b4e615f4352d68&utm

_source=Newsletter&utm_term=Girls%20%20Sex.

Interpol. "'Sextortion' Questions and Answers."
    Retrieved September 1, 2016. http://www
    .mensenhandelweb.nl/en/system/files/documents
    /26%20okt%202015/26%201.pdf.

Jackman, Tom. "'Sextortion, Growing Online Problem
    Worldwide, Victimizes Two George Mason Stu-
    dents." Washington Post, May 10, 2016. https://www.
    washingtonpost.com/news/true-crime/wp/2016/05
    /10/sextortion-growing-online-problem-worldwide
    -victimizes-two-george-mason-students.

Myers, Lysa. "Tips for Protecting Against Extortion." We
    Live Security, March 17, 2014. http://www
    .welivesecurity.com/2014/03/17/tips-for-protecting
    -against-sextortion.

NetSafe. "Webcam Safety: Avoiding Sextortion and
    Blackmail." October 13, 2015. https://www
    .netsafe.org.nz/webcam-safety-avoiding-sextortion
    -and-blackmail.

Shontell, Alyson. "Miss Teen USA Was 'in Tears and
    Shock' After a Hacker Took Nude Photos Through
    Her Bedroom Webcam." Business Insider, May 23,
    2014. http://www.businessinsider.com/cassidy-wolf
    -discusses-the-hacker-who-captured-nude-photos
    -of-her-via-webcam-2014-5.

Smith, Rohan. "New Research Sheds Light on Tragic,
    Public Suicide of Sextortion Victim Amanda Todd."
    News.com Australia. May 14, 2016. http://www
    .news.com.au/lifestyle/real-life/new-research
    -sheds-light-on-tragic-public-suicide-of-sextortion
    -victim-amanda-todd/news-story/d1ea63aa8e744c8

68212c72479daced9.

United States Federal Bureau of Investigation. "What is Sextortion?" Retrieved September 1, 2016. https://www.fbi.gov/video-repository/newss-what-is-sextortion/view.

United States Department of Justice. "The National Strategy for Child Exploitation Prevention and Interdiction: A Report to Congress." April 16, 2016. https://www.justice.gov/psc/file/842411/download.

Van Zandt, Clint. "Internet 'Sextortionists' Target our Children." Newsvine, April 10, 2012. http://clintvanzandt.newsvine.com/_news/2012/04/10/11119270-internet-sextortionists-target-our-children.

Wittes, Benjamin, Clara Spera, Cody Poplin, and Quinta Jurecic. "Sextortion: Cybersecurity, Teenagers, and Remote Sexual Assault." Brookings, May 11, 2016. https://www.brookings.edu/research/sextortion-cybersecurity-teenagers-and-remote-sexual-assault.

INDEX

ABOUT THE AUTHOR

Avery Elizabeth Hurt is the author of many books for kids and young adults, including such diverse titles as *Cross-Cultural Etiquette* and *Ancient Chinese Government and Geography.* She spends a great deal of time online and uses social media both for work and for keeping up with far-flung friends and relatives.

PHOTO CREDITS

Cover Marcos Mesa Sam Wordley/Shutterstock.com; back cover photo by Marianna armata/Moment/Getty Images; p. 5 Randy Brooke/WireImage/Getty Images; pp. 7, 16, 29, 40 (background) A. and I. Kruk/Shutterstock.com; p. 8 Peter Dazeley/The Image Bank/Getty Images; p. 9 filadendron/E+/ Getty Images; p. 12 Archive Photos/Getty Images; p. 14 Daniel Knighton/WireImage/Getty Images; p. 17 PeopleImages /DigitalVision/Getty Images; p. 20 Chinnapong/Shutterstock .com; p. 21 Ivan Afanasev/Shutterstock.com; p. 23 Focus and Blur/Shutterstock.com; p. 26 loginovworkshop/Shutterstock .com; p. 30 Photographee.eu/Shutterstock.com; p. 32 Andressa Anholete/AFP/Getty Images; p. 34 Ariel Skelley/Blend Images /Getty Images; p. 36 South_agency/E+/Getty Images; p. 41 Richard Hutchings/Corbis Documentary/Getty Images; pp. 44–45 Alex Wong/Getty Images; p. 47 Bryan Bedder/Getty Images; p. 50 Rob Marmion/Shutterstock.com.

Design: Michael Moy; Layout Design: Tahara Anderson; Editor: Bernadette Davis; Photo Researcher: Nicole Baker

$25.85

LONGWOOD PUBLIC LIBRARY
800 Middle Country Road
Middle Island, NY 11953
(631) 924-6400
longwoodlibrary.org

LIBRARY HOURS

Monday-Friday	9:30 a.m. - 9:00 p.m.
Saturday	9:30 a.m. - 5:00 p.m.
Sunday (Sept-June)	1:00 p.m. - 5:00 p.m.